In Memory
Of
Lincoln Meeks

www.SUDC.org

Sudden Unexplained Death in Childhood

Perfectly Imperfect Family

Illustrated by
Natia Gogiashvili

Written by
Amie Lands

Thirty-Three Press

Illustrated by Natia Gogiashvili
Edited by Bridgett Harris
Cover Design by Fresh Design

ISBN 978-1-7334818-0-9 (Paperback),
978-1-7334818-1-6 (Hardback),
978-1-7334818-2-3 (Ebook)

Library of Congress Control Number: 2019913478

Printed in the United States of America

First Printing, 2019

For bulk or wholesale ordering, contact the author.
www.amielandsauthor.com

To my amazing boys, Reid & Adam.

In memory of their beautiful sister, Ruthie Lou.

I have a perfectly imperfect family.

I have a mom and dad, and a little brother, too. My mom and dad love us and they love each other very much.

I also have a sister.
I never met her because she
died before I was born.

My mom and dad love sister as much as they love us. Even though she isn't here with us, she is always part of our family.

Pictures of sister hang on the walls around our house. We read her books and play with her toys. It's what siblings do.

We're always sure to include
sister on our special days.

At Thanksgiving, we share what we are thankful for in honor of her.

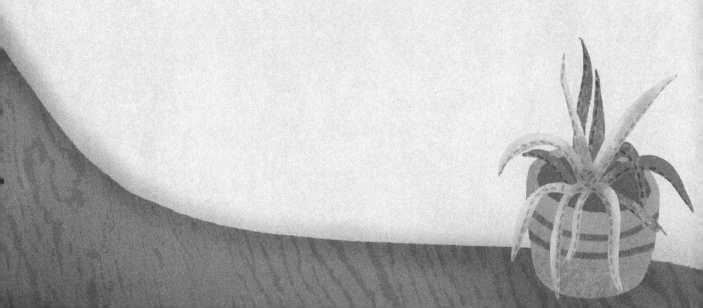

At Christmas, we hang her
stocking next to ours.

On my birthday, we invite friends over to eat cake while we open presents.

On sister's birthday we eat cake, too. Then we release ladybugs and send her our love.

I think about my sister and wonder what she would have been like.

My parents tell me that they loved her so much. That's how they knew they would love me so much, too.

I love my sister because she put so much love into my parents' hearts.

I have a perfectly imperfect family. My mom, dad, and brother here with me, and my sister always in my heart.

All About MY Family

We have five people in our family.

Their names are Chris, Amie, Ruthie Lou, Reid & Adam.

Something special about my sister is she had auburn hair like my dad's beard & she lived for 33 days.

We include our sister on special occasions by buying a gift for a child in need at Christmas. We light a candle at the Thanksgiving table. On her birthday, we eat delicious food all day!

All About YOUR Family

We have _____ people in our family.

Their names are _____

_____

Something special about my _____is_____

_____

We include _____ on special occasions by

_____

_____

_____

Amie Lands is a teacher, wife, and mama to three beautiful children. She is the author of Navigating the Unknown and Our Only Time. Since her daughter Ruthie Lou's brief life, Amie's passion is providing support and offering hope to bereaved families. She is the proud founder of The Ruthie Lou Foundation and a Certified Grief Recovery Specialist®. Amie lives in California with her husband, their two sons, and the family dog.

Natia Gogiashvili is an illustrator, wife, and mother of one little boy. In 2010, she began working with authors to create children's books. Natia and her family live in Georgia.

CPSIA information can be obtained
at www.ICGtesting.com
Printed in the USA
LVHW070033040820
662331LV00032B/548